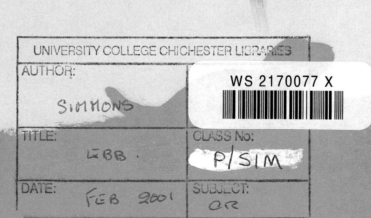

Ebb and Flo and the Baby Seal

Jane Simmons

 ORCHARD BOOKS

For Cordy, Miggy and Max

ORCHARD BOOKS
96 Leonard Street, London EC2A 4XD
Orchard Books Australia
14 Mars Road, Lane Cove, NSW 2066
1 84121 461 2
First published in Great Britain in 2000
Copyright © Jane Simmons 2000
The right of Jane Simmons to be identified as the author and illustrator of this work has been
asserted by her in accordance with the Copyright, Designs and Patents Act, 1988.
A CIP catalogue record for this book is available from the British Library.
1 3 5 7 9 10 8 6 4 2
Printed in Singapore

Ebb sat and listened to the rain and the wind.
Pitter, patter, pitter, patter, pitter, patter, woosh!

Ebb had eaten all her biscuits
and chewed her toy into little bits.
She wanted someone to play with.
"Woof!" said Ebb, but Flo was
busy painting.

"Woof!" said Ebb, but Bird was busy
chatting with the ducks.
"Woof!" said Ebb, but Mum was busy too.

So Ebb sat and listened to the wind and the rain.

Pitter, patter, pitter, patter, pitter, patter, woosh!

Then she heard a cry from the beach. "Wah! Wah!"

It was a baby seal! At last Ebb
had someone to play with.
They played on the sand.

They played in the waves.

They played in
the rockpools.

Ebb and the baby seal
played all day long.

As it got later, Ebb thought of her dinner.
But when she set off for home, the baby
seal tried to follow.

"Wah! Wah!" cried the baby seal.

Ebb stopped. "Woof!" she barked.
Why wouldn't the baby seal go home?
Ebb went to fetch help.

"Woof!" barked Ebb.
"Beep!" said Bird.
"Shush!" said Mum. "We're busy!"
"Woof! WOOF!" barked Ebb again, even louder.

"What's the matter,
Ebb?" said Flo.
"WOOF! WOOF! WOOF!"
went Ebb until Flo and
Mum followed her . . .

. . . all the way down to the beach.
"It's a baby seal," said Flo.
"Maybe she's hungry."
"Maybe she's lost," said Mum.

"Wah! Wah!" cried the baby seal.
"She needs her mum!" said Flo.
"And I know where to find her,"
said Mum. "Follow me!"

Flo followed Mum, Ebb followed Flo,
and the baby seal followed Ebb.
"Wah!" went the baby seal.

Flo heaved on the oars as
Mum pushed off.
"Woof!" said Ebb to the
baby seal.
"Wah!" the baby seal
cried back.

They rowed all the way out to
Seal Island.
"Woof! Woof!" barked Ebb.
"Wah!" went the baby seal.

There were seals everywhere.
"Oh no!" said Flo. "We'll
never find her mum!"
Ebb looked out to sea.

Suddenly Ebb saw a head
bobbing all alone.
   "Woof! Woof! WOOF!" Ebb
barked as loud as she could.
   Then they heard a loud "HOO!"
   "Wah!" answered the baby seal.
   "Ebb, you've found her mum!"
said Flo.

The baby seal and her mother played together.
"Well done, Ebb," said Flo.
"Woof!" said Ebb.
"Waah! Hoo!" said the seals.
"Let's go home," said Mum.

That night, Ebb dreamed of the sea
and boats and seals. *Pitter patter,*
pitter, patter, pitter, patter, woosh!
And far away there came a *Wah! Hoo!* . . .
but Ebb was fast asleep.